Hummingbirds

SHEILA McCULLAGH

The Ivory Dragon

Drawings by Tony Morris

Collins Educational

The Ivory Dragon

Peter was crossing the little bridge over the canal, on his way home from school. He was looking down, and going very carefully, because he was carrying a big box with two gerbils in it. The box was made of wood, with glass in one side, so that the gerbils could see out and Peter could see in. There were little holes in the top of the box, to let air in. He wanted to show the gerbils to Joe, before he went home.

He stopped on the bridge for a few moments, and looked down into the water. The canal was a very small one. It ran between the factories and houses of the city where Peter lived, and the water was brown and dirty. But he always stopped to watch the way the light shone on the water, and the ripples made lines out from an old post.

"Look who's here," someone shouted.

Peter looked up. Two boys were coming over the bridge. He knew the boys. They lived in a house at the end of his street. They were both older than he was, and he didn't like them. The bigger boy was called Gary. The other boy was called Jack.

"What have you got there, then?" asked Gary, coming up to him.

"Gerbils," said Peter.

"Mice," said Jack, peering into the box. "What do you want to take mice home for? I bet you've lots of mice running around in your house now!"

"Dirty, that's what they are," said Gary.

"They're not!" said Peter. "They're gerbils, and they're all right."

"There's only one thing to do with mice," said Jack, "and that's drown them. Throw them into the canal."

Gary grabbed the box.

"Don't touch them!" cried Peter. "Leave them alone!"

Gary jerked the box out of his hands.

"Give it back," shouted Peter, grabbing the box again. "They're gerbils. They're mine."

Jack kicked Peter's ankle, and hit him in the face. As Peter fell down, Gary tossed the box over the wall into the river.

"Don't bring any of your dirty little mice into our street again," he said.

Jack laughed, and the two of them walked on.

Peter scrambled to his feet and looked over into the river. The box was still floating, glass side up. It was two or three feet from the bank. Peter could see that it was beginning to fill with water. He ran across the bridge and along the bank towards it. He dropped down and lay flat on the bank, and tried to reach it. But the box was just out of reach.

"I'll get it, Peter," someone shouted.

He looked sideways. Joe was running along the bank. He had a stick in his hands. He dropped down beside Peter and reached out over the water. The stick touched the box. The box bobbed up and down. Joe slid the stick along to the corner of the box, and began to push. Slowly, the box came in nearer the bank. As soon as it was within reach, Peter grabbed one end of it. Joe dropped the stick, and grabbed the other. Peter could see the two little gerbils inside, clinging to the sides of the box, just above the water.

It was all the boys could do to heave the box slowly up and out. As they heaved, the water poured out of the cracks in the box.

They hung over the bank, almost falling in themselves, until at last, with another big heave, they got the box up and on to the pavement.

"Thanks," said Peter. "I'd never have got it out."

"What are they?" asked Joe.

"Gerbils," said Peter. "I got them in the market."

"They look all right," said Joe.

"They live in deserts," said Peter. "They must hate water."

"I'll help you get them home," said Joe. "Bring them to our house. I've got a big tin there. We could put them in that, while the box dries out."

They carried the dripping box along between them, and turned into John Street, where they both lived.

They stopped at Joe's house. Joe pulled out a key.

"No one's home yet," he said, opening the door. "Come on."

They took the box into the kitchen. Joe got a big tin from a shed in the back yard. They tore up some dry newspaper to put in it, and then Peter took the gerbils out of the wet box. He dried them off as well as he could with his handkerchief, and put them in the tin. Then he washed his face and hands. He brushed the mud off his coat, so that he would look all right when his mother saw him. She was always a bit upset, if he had a fight.

"I'd better get on home," he said to Joe. "I'm late,"

"Have a look at the fireworks before you go," said Joe. "I've got another rocket. A big one. A seven-star rocket."

Joe and Peter were collecting fireworks for bonfire night. They were going to let them off in Joe's back yard. They had been saving up for them for weeks.

They went out to the yard. They were keeping the fireworks in the shed. (Joe's mother was afraid of fire, and she wouldn't have them in the house.) There were a good many fireworks now, in the cardboard boxes on the shelf. The new rocket was a big one. Joe was very pleased with it. So was Peter.

They counted the fireworks again. They had put them in the order in which they were going to let them off, but they changed the order almost every day.

"Where shall we put the big rocket?" asked Peter.

"Let's start with it," said Joe. "Let's start with a big bang and a shower of stars."

They put the rocket in the first box.

Peter picked up the tin with the gerbils and they went over the road to Peter's house. Joe carried the wet box. Peter could hear someone talking in the kitchen. "We must have a visitor," he said, as he opened the door.

"I'll get back, then," said Joe.

Peter took the box. "Thanks," he said.

Joe ran off, and Peter slipped in and up to his room with the wet box and the big tin.

He took a quick look in the mirror. His cheek was a bit red, where Jack had hit him, but he didn't look too bad. He looked in the tin. The gerbils had hidden themselves under the torn paper. He pulled a carrot out of his pocket, and dropped it into the tin. There were holes in the lid, so he put it on carefully, and put the tin down on the table by his bed.

Then he took another quick look in the mirror, brushed a lump of mud off his coat, and ran downstairs. He opened the door, and went into the kitchen.

A strange man was sitting in a chair by the fire. He looked up as Peter opened the door. He had thick white hair, and he was wearing a navy blue sweater.

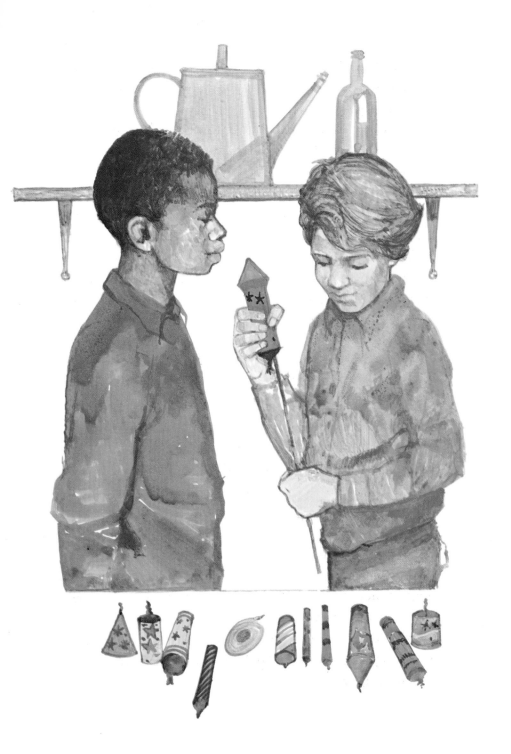

"Come in and shut the door, Peter," said his mother. She handed the stranger a cup of tea. "This is your Great-Uncle Davy."

Great-Uncle Davy! Peter remembered hearing about him since he was very small. He had never seen him before. Great-Uncle Davy was always away. He seemed to get on a ship, and travel across the world, as easily as Peter got on a 'bus and went into the town. Sometimes they had a postcard from some far away country, but Great-Uncle Davy hadn't been home for years. The last time was long before Peter was born. Now he sat there on the other side of the kitchen fire, drinking his tea and smoking an old pipe.

"Well, Peter," he said with a nod. "How are you?"

"All right," said Peter.

"You've been fighting again," said his mother, looking at his face. "Oh, Peter. I wish you'd keep away from those boys."

"He doesn't look much hurt," said Great-Uncle Davy. "You have to fight now and then, if you're a boy."

"I can't think why," said his mother.

Great-Uncle Davy blew out a cloud of smoke, and settled himself back in his chair. Peter couldn't take his eyes off him. His face was brown, from being out in the sun and wind. His eyes were dark, with lines at the corners, as if he was used to looking out a long way over the sea. His hands looked as if he was used to doing a hard day's work.

"Uncle Davy's staying the night," said his mother. "But he has to go very early in the morning. He's given us a present. Look!"

She put a small, carved, white dragon on the table.

Peter picked it up. He had never seen anything like it before.

It was a wonderful carving. Every bone on the dragon's back, every line of its body, had been carved out. The dragon's eyes almost seemed to be watching him. Its mouth was open, as if it were breathing invisible fire. It had curled its body round, as if it was going to shoot off into the air.

"Where did it come from?" asked Peter.

"I got it in the east, on the other side of the world," said Great-Uncle Davy. "I bought it from an old man, who lived up in the mountains."

"What's it made of?" asked Peter.

"Ivory," said Great-Uncle Davy. "At least, that's what it is *now*. But the old man told me a long story about it. He said that once, long, long ago, it was a real dragon. It was a hundred times as big as it is now, and it lived in a cave, up in the mountains.

"There was a village down in the valley, and the dragon used to fly down at night, when the moon was shining. The villagers were very frightened of the dragon. They said the dragon sometimes stole a sheep, but I don't know about that.

"An old man came to the village one night, and asked for shelter. The villagers took him in, and gave him food, and a warm bed. The villagers didn't know it, but the old man was a magician.

"There was a full moon that night, and the dragon flew down from the mountains, as he always did when the moon was full. He flew over the village, breathing fire and smoke, and frightening everyone. The magician saw him, and made a spell. He turned him into a little ivory dragon, who could do no harm at all.

"The magician took the ivory dragon with him the next morning, when he left the village. He sold him in the nearest

market. But when he sold the dragon, the magician warned the man who bought him. 'This is a real dragon,' he said. 'But he is under a spell. You must never let the dragon see moonstones; for if he sees a moonstone, he will be able to eat it, and if the dragon eats even one moonstone, the spell will be broken. The dragon will still be an ivory dragon by day, but he will come alive again by night, and fly about as he used to do, whenever the moon is shining. If he eats more than one moonstone, he will begin to grow. If he eats seven moonstones, he will grow to his full size. Even then, he will only be alive at night. During the daytime he will still be a little ivory dragon. But then, if someone shakes the petals of five white roses over him, the dragon will be himself again, by day as well as by night. He will fly back to his cave in the mountains, even if he has to fly half-way across the world.' "

There was silence for a moment. Then Peter's mother laughed. "You've learnt some tales in your travels, Uncle Davy," she said.

"I'm only telling you what the old man told me," said Great-Uncle Davy. "It all happened long, long ago, and many people have owned the ivory dragon since then. But whenever anyone has sold the ivory dragon, he has always passed on the magician's warning. So I'm passing it on to you."

"Well, if I believed you, I wouldn't have the dragon in the house," said his mother. "Don't you remember giving me some moonstones as a wedding present? I've still got them upstairs, in a little ivory box."

"I'd forgotten that," said Great-Uncle Davy. "Well, keep your moonstones in the ivory box, and don't let the dragon see them. Then you'll be all right. How do you like the dragon, Peter?"

Peter was sitting staring at the little ivory dragon. Was it just the fire-light flickering, or had the dragon moved, when his mother said she had the moonstones? For a moment, Peter thought the dragon's eyes were shining.

"He looks alive now," he said.

"It's just a story, Peter," said his mother. "Uncle Davy talks a lot of nonsense sometimes."

Great-Uncle Davy laughed. "Yes, it's just a story," he said. "But it's not nonsense. I've been in many strange places, and I've seen many strange things happen. I shouldn't let the dragon see those moonstones, if I were you."

*   *   *

When Peter got up in the morning Great-Uncle Davy was gone. He had left very early to catch a train.

"He's only just got home, and yet he's gone off on another of his travels," said Peter's mother. "He's leaving by ship tonight, and he doesn't know when he'll be back."

"I'd like to travel like that," said Peter.

"Well I wouldn't," said his mother. "Not the way Uncle Davy does. He's never at home. He hasn't got a home. He just wanders about."

Peter finished his breakfast, and took another carrot upstairs for the gerbils. They were making a nest in the paper, and they seemed none the worse for their swim the day before.

The box had dried out overnight. He tore up some more paper for the box, and took the gerbils out of the tin. They had far more room in the big wooden box, and they seemed glad to be back in it. Peter watched them exploring the box, until he had to set off for school.

He had just got outside the house, when he saw Mrs. Bell's cat. Mrs. Bell lived next door. She lived all alone, and she had a big black and white cat called Rags.

Rags was creeping along by the wall, after a bird.

"Shoo! Get off!" shouted Peter, waving his arms at it.

The cat jumped round, and the bird flew off, and Mrs. Bell shot out of her house.

"What are you yelling at Rags for?" she cried. "Don't you dare yell at my cat like that! You'll be throwing stones at him next. I know you! And I won't have it!"

"But he was after a bird," said Peter.

"Don't you talk to me about birds," said Mrs. Bell, picking Rags up. "You leave my cat alone. I won't have it, I tell you."

She shot back into the house, with Rags in her arms, and slammed the door.

"I didn't touch the cat," Peter said to the door. It was no good. His mother told him to be nice to Mrs. Bell, because she lived alone. But Mrs. Bell didn't want him to be nice to her. It was better to keep out of her way.

He saw Joe across the street. He ran over to him, and they set off for school together.

*   *   *

When Peter got back that afternoon, his mother was out. The ivory dragon was on the table. So was a little ivory box, and six small, flat, round stones, that looked a bit like glass buttons, with no holes in them. He picked one up.

He was looking at the stone, when his mother came in.

"Back already, Peter?" she cried. "I was sure I'd get home before you did."

"What are these?" asked Peter.

"Those are the moonstones," said his mother, taking off her coat. "Mrs. Brown came in, and I was showing them to her."

"But—but the dragon's here!" cried Peter. "He's seen them."

"I was showing her the dragon, too," said his mother. She laughed. "You don't believe that story your Uncle Davy told us, do you?" she said.

"I don't know," said Peter. "How many moonstones did Uncle Davy give you?"

"I think there were seven," said his mother, coming to the table.

"There are only six now," said Peter.

"There must be one more," said his mother. "See if it's dropped on the floor."

Peter looked on the floor below the table. There was no moonstone there. He looked all around, but there was no moonstone.

"It's not here," he said.

"Are you sure?" asked his mother. "Oh, well. There may have been only six to begin with. I thought there were seven, but I don't remember. But you can see that it's all right, and the dragon is just an ivory dragon. It was only a story that Uncle Davy told you. Uncle Davy knows all kinds of strange stories."

Peter looked at the ivory dragon. It stood there on its black stand, with its body curled, ready for a spring, just as it had always done. And yet he was sure that there was something different about it. The dragon's eyes were shining.

"I'll put the rest of the moonstones away," he said. He picked them up, and put them in the little ivory box.

"Take them up to my room," said his mother.

Peter picked up the moonstones. The dragon seemed to be watching him, as he put the moonstones back in their box, and left the room.

*   *   *

After tea, Peter had another look at the gerbils. They were getting to know him, and they sat on his hands and ran up his arm. He played with them for some time, before he got into bed.

He had been asleep for hours, when he heard a wild howl outside. He leapt out of bed, and ran to the window. Something white flew past in the moonlight, with a flash of fire. There was another howl from below. Peter looked down.

A big black and white cat was running along the top of the wall in the moonlight, howling. It's fur was on fire on one side. As Peter looked, it jumped down off the wall into the water barrel which stood outside Mrs. Bell's back door. The barrel was full of water, and the fire went out. The cat splashed wildly, clawed its way up over the side of the barrel, and jumped down. It was still howling, as it ran off into the darkness.

Peter sat down on the side of his bed, and stared out of the window. The moon was shining down on the back yards of the houses. The moon wouldn't be full till Saturday, bonfire night, but it seemed almost as bright as day outside. There were no lights in any of the windows. No one else had heard the cat. No one else had seen what happened.

He shivered with excitement. Then, as he sat watching, he saw another flash of fire, and something white flew past the window. It was long, like a snake, but it was much thicker than a snake.

"The dragon!" said Peter softly. "The ivory dragon! He's alive!"

He waited for some time at the window, looking out, but the dragon had gone, and he began to feel very cold. He climbed slowly back into bed, and pulled up the blankets. It was a long time before he got back to sleep.

*   *   *

There was a bang on the door when they were having breakfast next morning, and Mrs. Bell burst in, with Rags in her arms.

"What's up?" asked Peter's father, looking up. "Something wrong with the cat?"

"Yes, there is something wrong," cried Mrs. Bell. "And what I want to know is, what does Peter know about it?"

"Peter?" asked his mother. "Why should Peter know anything?"

"He was yelling at my cat the other day," said Mrs. Bell. "I shouldn't wonder if he was throwing stones at it. And look at it now!"

She held out the cat. Its fur was burnt all down one side.

"Someone set it on fire," she said. "Or it was one of those nasty fireworks. I've seen him with those fireworks."

"I didn't," said Peter. "I didn't hurt it."

"Somebody did," said Mrs. Bell.

"Well it wasn't Peter," said his father. "Peter likes animals. He wouldn't do a thing like that. You can't go round saying things like that about Peter, Mrs. Bell."

"You see that he leaves my cat alone, that's all!" cried Mrs. Bell. She turned round and went out, banging the door behind her.

"I'm fed up with that woman," said Peter's father. "I don't know why you have anything to do with her."

"She's lonely," said his mother. "She lives all alone, and that cat is the only thing she's got to care about."

"I don't wonder she's lonely, when she behaves like that," said his father. "Peter would never touch her cat, would you, Peter?"

"It was the dragon," said Peter. "I'm sure it was. I saw him last night, outside the window. The dragon flew past, and then the cat ran along the wall, with its fur on fire."

"You've been dreaming again, Peter," said his mother. "I shall be sorry Uncle Davy gave us the dragon, if it gives you bad dreams."

"It wasn't a dream," said Peter.

"It must have been," said his father. He picked the dragon up and looked at it. "It's a good bit of work. It *does* look real, in a way. But it's made of ivory, Peter. It can't fly."

"You'd better hurry up, or you'll be late for school," said his mother. "Get your coat. I want you to call in at the shop for me on your way home, for some apples. Here's the money. Off you go now."

Peter got his coat, and set off for school.

He was thinking so much about the dragon, that he got into trouble three or four times that day for day-dreaming when he should have been listening.

In the last part of the afternoon they were painting pictures. Peter painted a picture of a great white dragon, with fiery red eyes, and long claws. The dragon was flying through the night, and the sky above him shone with stars. Peter was thinking so hard about the dragon, that he didn't notice the time. As he finished his picture, he saw that everyone else had cleared up. Mr. Brent, his teacher, came over to look at the picture.

"What is it this time, Peter?" asked Mr. Brent. "A dragon?

You're always painting monsters. I wish you'd have a go at painting something real—something you can look at, and touch."

Mr. Brent looked at the picture more closely.

"It's a magnificent dragon, Peter," he said. "I must say that. I think it's the best thing you've ever done. It almost looks as if it were alive. It's got a strange look about the eyes, too. It looks as if the dragon is watching you. 'Magnificent' is the only word for it. A magnificent dragon. But I'd like you to try something that wasn't a monster next time. Something real."

"It is real," said Peter. "It's a real dragon. We've got one at home. He looks like ivory, but once he was a real dragon, and _____."

The bell went.

"There's no more time, Peter," said Mr. Brent. "You've still got to clear up your things. Be quick, or you'll be late home. Leave your picture on the side to dry, and think about what I said. Paint something real, next time."

Peter cleared up as quickly as he could, but he was late. He almost forgot the apples, and had to go back for them, so that it was quite dark by the time he got home.

He looked for the dragon as soon as he got in, but it wasn't on the table. There were cupboards on one side of the fireplace, with shelves over them. His mother had put the dragon on the very top shelf. He pulled a chair over to the shelves. He was standing on the chair, looking at the dragon, when his mother came in.

"Now then," she said. "You leave that dragon alone. If you have any more bad dreams, we'll get rid of it. Help me set the table. Do you want one of the apples for your gerbils? Joe looked in a few minutes ago. He wants you to go round and see him after tea. He seemed a bit upset about something. I think you'd better go, but I don't want you out late, these dark nights."

Peter's father came in, and they had tea. Peter finished his as quickly as he could. He cut a bit off one of the apples, and took it up to the gerbils in his room. Then he ran downstairs, and went across the street to see Joe.

"Come on out to the shed," said Joe, when he opened the door and saw Peter. "Someone's pinched our fireworks."

"What!" cried Peter.

"Come and see," said Joe.

They went out to the shed. Joe lit a candle.

"Look!" he said.

The shelf at the back of the shed was empty. The fireworks were gone.

Peter stared at the empty shelf for a moment in silence. He couldn't believe that the fireworks were not there. They had been saving up for them for weeks. Last weekend they had gone out with Bill's dad, and they had spent the whole of Saturday afternoon buying them. They would never get the money for any more in time for bonfire night.

"Do you know who pinched them?" he asked at last.

"I don't *know*, but I've a good idea," said Joe. "I met Jack on the way back from school. He asked me what we were doing on bonfire night. He was grinning about something."

"What did your Dad say?" asked Peter.

"I didn't tell him," said Joe. "And I'm not going to. Gary and Jack would be worse than ever, if I told anyone. We'll have to go and watch the ones in the park."

*   *   *

Peter lay awake a long time, after he went to bed that night, thinking about the fireworks, but at last he dropped off to sleep.

A puff of smoke drifted under the door, and into his room.

Peter woke with a start. The moon was shining in on his face. There was a smell of burning in the air. He jumped out of bed, and opened the door.

The dragon was at the door of his parents' room. He was trying to get in. He was breathing fire, and the floor on the landing was smoking. As Peter looked, a little flame of fire shot up from the wood.

"Stop it!" cried Peter. "You'll burn the house down!"

There was a flash of white, and a puff of fire, and the dragon was gone, flying back down the stairs towards the kitchen.

Peter picked up a mat and threw it over the flames.

"Peter! What's burning?" cried his father, pulling open the door of his room.

Peter bent down, and pulled the mat back. The fire was out.

"It was the dragon," said Peter. "He's after those moonstones. He was trying to get in your door, and he set the floor on fire."

"Peter!" said his mother, coming to the door. "Oh, Peter, you've been dreaming again."

"I'm glad he was dreaming," said his father. "Look at the floor. The whole house could have been burnt down."

"You must have dropped a cigarette end," said Peter's mother. "I'm always telling you to stop smoking. It's bad for you. And now look what you've done! We might have been burnt in our beds."

"It wasn't Dad's cigarette. It was the dragon," said Peter. "When he's alive at night, he breathes fire. I've seen him before."

"Now, Peter, you go back to bed," said his mother. "We'll get rid of that dragon if it gives you bad dreams. I'm going down to make a cup of tea."

She went downstairs. Peter slipped back into bed.

"Was the dragon in the kitchen?" he asked, when his mother came in a few minutes later, with a cup in her hand.

"Yes, it was," she said. "Where else do you think it would be? It was on the top shelf, where I left it. Here's some hot milk. I'll put out the light now. The moon's so bright, you don't need any light. You go back to sleep, as soon as you've had your milk, and forget about that dragon."

Peter drank the milk slowly. He was sure that the dragon must have been after the moonstones. The dragon wanted to grow. What would happen if he grew to his full size? He remembered what Great-Uncle Davy had said about the white roses. What would happen if he shook the petals of five white roses over the dragon now, while he was still small? Would he fly back to his own country?

Peter put his empty cup down on the floor, and lay there, thinking about the dragon, until at last he fell asleep.

*   *   *

When he got home from school next day, the dragon wasn't there. His mother saw him looking at the empty shelf.

"It's gone," she said. "I took it up to Mr. Day myself, first thing." (Mr. Day kept the shop at the end of the street. Peter's father called it 'the junk shop', but Mr. Day had some very old and strange things in it.) "Your father is going to call in the shop on his way back from work, and see what he'll give us for it."

"I wish he hadn't gone," said Peter.

24

"I won't have anything in this house that gives you bad dreams," said his mother.

"They're not bad dreams," said Peter. "I'm not frightened of the dragon. I'm sorry for him, in a way. He only wants to go back to his cave in the mountain."

"You're as bad as your Uncle Davy, making up tales about dragons," said his mother.

Peter said nothing. He knew that his mother would never believe the dragon was alive; unless she saw him herself.

The room seemed empty without the dragon. When his father came home, he asked him what Mr. Day had said.

"Mr. Day is going to have the dragon valued," said his father. "You can say what you like about Mr. Day, but he's fair. He says it's really old. It's got to be valued, so that he can give us a fair price for it."

"What will Great-Uncle Davy say, when he knows we've sold it?" asked Peter.

"We hadn't seen Great-Uncle Davy for fifteen years, till he dropped in the other day," said his mother. "I expect it will be another fifteen years before he comes again. And I'm sure he wouldn't mind us selling the dragon, if he knew that it gave you bad dreams."

*   *   *

Peter spent some time watching his gerbils, before he went to sleep. They were settling down very well, and he decided that he would get some more boxes, and make a long run for them. Perhaps the gerbils were safer, now that the dragon had gone. If the dragon had stolen a sheep from the village on the mountain when he was full size, he might try to eat a gerbil, when he was only small. Peter made sure that his window was open only a little way, before he finally got into bed, and went to sleep.

He woke to find the moonlight streaming into his room. He sat up in bed. Something had woken him. What was it?

He listened.

There was a strange sound at the window, as if someone was trying to get in. There was a knock on the glass.

Peter jumped out of bed, and ran over to the window.

The little dragon was outside on the sill, trying to push up the window. His eyes were shining, and he looked very much alive.

This time, he didn't fly off when he saw Peter. He stopped trying to push up the window, and stood quite still.

Peter stood staring at him. As he watched, a little puff of fire came out of the dragon's mouth, and he heard someone whisper his name.

"Peter!" came the whisper. "Peter!"

It was the dragon.

"What do you want?" asked Peter. "You're not after my gerbils, are you?"

"Of course not," whispered the dragon. "I only eat moonstones. Let me in. Let me in. I want to talk to you."

"I'm not going to let you in," said Peter. "You've come for the moonstones, and if you eat those, you'll grow."

"No, I haven't," said the dragon. "I've got moonstones. I've got as many as I need, in the shop. There's a bag of moonstones there. I've come to see you. Let me in."

Peter pushed the window up a little way, and the dragon slipped under it into the room. He flew on to the little table by Peter's bed. He didn't even look at the gerbils.

"Peter," said the dragon. "I've found all the moonstones I need. But I haven't eaten them yet, because I wanted to see you. I thought you'd be afraid of me, if I was my full size. Don't be afraid. I won't hurt you."

"I'm not afraid," said Peter.

"Good," whispered the dragon. Every time he spoke, a little puff of fire blew out of his mouth, but Peter saw that he was being careful not to set anything alight.

"Peter," said the dragon, "I want you to help me to fly back to my cave in the mountains. You heard what your uncle said. Find five white roses for me, Peter, and shake the petals over me."

"But then you'll frighten the villagers again, and steal their sheep."

"No, I won't," said the dragon. "I don't eat sheep. I told you. I only eat moonstones. They lost one of the sheep, and said I'd taken it. But I shan't go near the village again. I don't want them to bring the magician back. I just want to be back in the mountains, to fly in the moonlight. It's wonderful to fly at night, Peter, under the full moon. If you get the white roses for me, I'll take you flying before I go. You can climb on my back and fly with me, with the stars over your head and the dark town below."

Peter looked at the little dragon. The dragon's eyes were fixed on him, and somehow he believed what the dragon said.

"I'll come back tomorrow night, Peter," whispered the dragon. "But I shall be my full size then. Don't be afraid. Get the roses. The moon will be full tomorrow night. We'll fly out over the town together. Then I'll bring you back here, and fly off to my mountains, on the other side of the world."

"All right," said Peter. "I'll get the white roses. There's a market tomorrow. I can get them there."

The dragon's eyes shone with delight, and a long flicker of flame came out of his mouth. "Home!" he whispered to himself. "Home to the mountains!" He flew across the room to the sill.

"Remember! I shall be my full size," he said. "You won't be afraid?"

Peter shook his head. "I'm not afraid," he said. "I'll get the roses."

Another long jet of fire flickered from the dragon's mouth. There was a flash of white, and he was gone.

Peter shut the window and went slowly back to bed.

*   *   *

The next day was Saturday and bonfire night.

Joe came over in the morning, when Peter was cleaning out the gerbils in the yard.

"I had to tell Dad someone pinched the fireworks," said Joe. "He wanted to know when we were going to let them off."

"Did you tell him it was Jack?" asked Peter.

"No, I didn't," said Joe. "And don't you tell him. I don't want Gary and Jack after me. Dad said he'd take me to the park, to see the fireworks there. Want to come?"

Peter shook his head. All the fun seemed to have gone out of bonfire night, now that the fireworks had been stolen. In any case, he was thinking about the dragon. He had even forgotten that it *was* bonfire night, until Joe had said so.

"Come over about six, if you change your mind," said Joe.

Peter went down to the market after tea. There was always a big market on Saturday, and he knew that his best chance of getting some roses cheap was to go down when everyone was clearing up. They sometimes had flowers left over. He hadn't much money. He and Joe had been spending everything they could get on fireworks. If he was going to buy roses in November, they had to be cheap.

Peter was lucky. There were some white roses left at the flower stall, and they didn't look very good ones. It was no wonder that they were still there.

"How much are they?" asked Peter, pointing to them.

"50p each," said the man at the flower stall.

His wife came round the back of the stall.

"Now then, don't be silly, Len," she said. "You know those roses will be no good by Monday. You can have the lot for 50p."

"I've only got 25," said Peter.

"They're worth more than that," said the man. "There's a dozen roses there."

"I only want five," said Peter.

"Oh, give them to him," said the woman. "They'll be no good on Monday. They're not much good now. I'm not taking them back with us now. Did you say you'd got 25p? Give it here, and you can have the lot."

Peter handed over the money, and took the roses.

He put them under his coat as he went into the house. He didn't want to have to tell anyone why he wanted them. But he met no one as he slipped upstairs to his room.

It was dark outside, and people were beginning to let off fireworks. He saw a rocket shoot up into the sky, and break into a cloud of stars. He wondered when the dragon would come.

Peter went to bed early, but he didn't get undressed. He lay down on the bed, waiting. He had left the curtains drawn back, and he lay watching the moon come up over the dark roofs of the houses. The window was open, and he could hear fireworks going off in the distance.

Suddenly, there was a bang at the window, and a bright light shone into the room.

Peter was out of bed in a moment, staring outside.

The dragon was there. His eyes were glowing like red coals, and a great flame of fire rolled out of his mouth. He had grown so much, that Peter could hardly believe it was the same dragon. He was at least six or seven metres long and his back shone like silver in the moonlight.

"Peter," breathed the dragon. Peter could tell that the dragon was trying to speak softly, but the words were a deep roar, rather than a whisper. "Peter. Have you got the white roses? The moon is up, and I'm ready to fly."

"I've got the roses," said Peter.

The dragon's eyes blazed like fires.

"Free!" he roared. "Free! I'm going home! Across the sea to the mountains, on the other side of the world!"

The dragon sprang up into the air, in sheer delight at the thought of being free. He swung round over the roofs of the houses, and glided down again to the window sill.

"Are you coming, Peter?" he roared. "Are you coming? Up into the air, and over the town, over the roofs and over the trees, over the chimneys and under the moon?"

Peter took a deep breath. His hands shook a little, but he was too excited to feel frightened. Besides, he had hidden the white roses in his cupboard, and he was sure that the dragon would bring him safely back for those. He pushed up the window, and swung his legs over the sill.

The dragon floated along the house until he lay in the air just beside the window sill, with his great head pointing down the lane at the back of the house.

Peter climbed out, and on to his back. The dragon's bones stuck out, and there were plenty of knobs for him to hold on to.

He had only just settled himself down, with one leg on each side of the dragon, and his hands gripping two knobs just behind the dragon's head, when a rocket shot up from a yard near by, and broke in a shower of red stars.

The dragon bounded up into the sky with a roar of delight. Puff after puff of fire burst from his mouth.

At first the dragon seemed to be dancing in the air with sheer delight at being free, and at being his full size again. He shot through the air as a live fish dives into the water, when a fisherman throws it back. It was all that Peter could do to hold on, while the dragon looped and whirled around the sky. Up he went towards the stars, like a great rocket. He swung round, and dived down towards the houses. Then up again, looping and whirling in the air.

But at last the dragon slowed down, and began a long, slow glide, high up over the roofs, and Peter could look down. He saw the whole city spread out below him. The houses looked like toys. Up and down and around they went, over the roofs and along the river, out to the park and round and back, high up over the city.

The dragon seemed delighted to see fireworks. Perhaps it was because his own breath was fire, but whenever a rocket shot up below them, the dragon dived down to watch the rocket break into stars.

There was a big patch of waste ground, farther down the canal, and Peter could see that someone had lit a bonfire there. The dragon was gliding towards it, watching the fire, when a very large rocket shot up from the waste ground, and burst into seven red stars just below them.

The dragon roared with delight, and dived down towards the bonfire. As they swept down out of the sky, Peter saw two boys standing by the fire. They had been letting off fireworks, but now they were staring up at the dragon. They seemed to be too frightened to move, as the dragon swept down. Peter saw their faces. They were Gary and Jack. Even in the firelight, he could see that their faces were white with fear. As the dragon shot towards them, they dropped the fireworks which they were holding, and fled, with wild cries, towards the houses. The dragon pulled himself out of his dive, and swept after them, three or four metres above the ground. As he overtook them, they flung themselves down on their faces in the mud. The dragon dipped down and then swept up high into the air again, swung round in a loop, and glided down over the river.

Peter laughed aloud. By this time, he was as excited as the dragon. The cold night air blew back his hair, and his hands gripped the knobs on the dragon's back. He was much too excited to feel frightened.

The dragon swung round, and glided back along the canal. They dropped lower, until they only just cleared the roofs of the houses.

As they came to the bridge over the river, Peter saw a man walking across it. The full moon was shining down, and it was almost as bright as day. A burst of star-shells lit up the ground below, and Peter saw who the man was. It was Mr. Brent.

As they glided towards the bridge, Mr. Brent looked up. He stopped dead, and stared. They were so close, that Peter saw Mr. Brent's mouth drop open with amazement. Then the dragon was across the bridge, gliding on and on through the air. Peter looked back. He could see Mr. Brent still standing on the bridge, staring after them.

Peter laughed again. "He'll know I painted something real, all right," he said to himself, as the dragon slowly turned over the roofs of the houses, back towards John Street.

Rags, the black and white cat, was walking slowly along the back wall, as the dragon glided towards the window of Peter's room. The dragon saw the cat, and let out a roar of rage. A great wave of fire shot out of his mouth towards Rags.

Rags looked up, saw the dragon, let out a howl of fear, and fled. The dragon just missed him, as he jumped down off the wall into darkness behind the dustbins. But the dragon's rush carried him over the back yards, up over the houses, and along John Street. Mrs. Bell was walking along the pavement, going home. She looked up and saw the dragon.

Mrs. Bell's howl was even louder than Rags'. She ran to her door, pulled it open, and fell into the house. As the dragon swung round towards Peter's house again, Mrs. Bell's door shut with a bang that echoed down the street.

Before the echoes had died away, the dragon had glided over the roof to the back yard. He stopped, floating gently in the air by the window of Peter's room.

"The roses, Peter! The white roses!" he whispered, in a voice that sounded like a rushing wind.

Peter climbed off the dragon's back and into his room. The roses were in a jar of water in his cupboard. He took them to the window. They were fully out and he was careful not to shake them.

He leant out over the sill, and held the roses over the dragon's back. The moon shone down. As he shook the flowers, the petals fell like large white snowflakes.

He saw the dragon shiver, as the petals of the roses touched his skin. Then, like a flash of white light, he shot up into the sky, higher and higher. In a few moments, he was so high up that he looked like a silver fish. And in a few moments more, he had gone.

Peter stood there, holding the stems of the roses in his hand. The petals had all fallen. He stood looking up into the sky, as the moon shone down. A rocket shot up, over the roof-tops, and burst into blue stars. Peter tossed the stems of the roses down into the yard. He shivered. For the first time that night he felt cold. He pushed the window down, and went to bed.

*   *   *

Peter woke the next morning to find the sun streaming in. He sat up in bed, and looked at the clock, ticking away on his table.

Eleven o'clock! He scrambled out of bed. It was Peter's job to go out and buy a Sunday paper, but his father must have got the paper himself by this time. Peter pulled on a heavy sweater, pushed his feet into his shoes, and went downstairs.

His mother was clearing the table.

"So you've woken up at last," she said. "I thought you were going to sleep all day. Did the fireworks keep you awake?"

"I saw some of the rockets," Peter said.

"That's what I told your dad. He got the paper himself this morning."

The paper was lying on the chair by the fire.

"Where is Dad?" asked Peter.

"Gone out again, up to the junk shop," said his mother. "The shop's in a fine old mess. Someone broke in there last night, and stole some things. Your dad met Mr. Day, when he went to get the paper. He's gone back to help him clear up a bit."

"What was stolen?" asked Peter.

"I don't know," said his mother. But the shop is in a terrible mess. Terrible, Dad said it was."

"Are there any moonstones missing?" asked Peter.

"You think about nothing but that story your Great-Uncle Davy told you," said his mother. "But you're right this time. Mr. Day *did* have some moonstones, and they've gone. And the ivory dragon was stolen, too, so you can forget all about it. It isn't there any longer. Come and have your cornflakes."

She put a bowl of cornflakes and a jug of milk on the table, and Peter sat down to eat them.

"I know you don't like Mr. Day," his mother went on. "He doesn't like boys in his shop. You can't be surprised at that. But he's a very fair man. He said that he'd pay us for the dragon. He said yesterday that he'd buy it. He was only wanting to have it valued. He can claim it on his insurance. You'll never guess what he's going to give us for it: a hundred pounds! What do you think of that?"

"It was a real dragon," said Peter. "It was worth it."

"You're as bad as your Great-Uncle Davy," said his mother. She poured some soup out into a bowl.

"Where are you taking the soup?" asked Peter, as his mother picked up the bowl, and went over to the door.

"I'm taking it to poor Mrs. Bell," said his mother. "I don't know what happened to her last night, but she's in ever such a bad way. She's in bed, and she's had the doctor—on Sunday morning, too! She said she was seeing things last night. She's ever so upset. She says she saw the devil. I don't know what's come over her. Don't laugh, Peter! She really is bad. You finish your breakfast."

She went out.

Peter hugged himself. He couldn't help laughing. He knew very well what Mrs. Bell had seen. He was sorry about the shop, but Mr. Day would never let him in to look round, in case he broke anything. He wondered how much damage the dragon had done. If the dragon had eaten the moonstones, and grown to his full size while he was still in the shop, the shop must be in a mess.

Peter helped himself to some more cornflakes.

*   *   *

Peter was a bit late in starting for school on Monday morning, and as he ran along towards the bridge, he saw Gary and Jack coming towards him. He stopped. He didn't want to meet them. But Gary and Jack didn't wait. They took one look at him, turned white, and ran off down a side street as fast as they could. Gary and Jack were frightened of him! Peter could scarcely believe it.

"But they're not frightened of me," he said to himself. "They're frightened of the dragon. I thought they saw me, when we swooped down on them last night."

He wondered what people would say, when Gary and Jack told them they had seen him riding a dragon. But, in a flash, he knew that Gary and Jack would never tell. They wouldn't dare to tell, because no one would believe them. No one would believe *him*, if he told them about the dragon. Joe might, but no one else would. And even Joe might say he was making it up.

"I don't care," he said to himself. "I know it happened, and so do Gary and Jack."

He ran on as fast as he could.

* * *

His class went to Mr. Brent's room again, at the end of the afternoon, to paint pictures. Mr. Brent was very interested in painting. He painted pictures himself. As soon as he went in, Peter saw that Mr. Brent had pinned his picture of the dragon up on the wall. Mr. Brent was standing looking at it.

"Hallo, Peter," he said. "I've been having another look at your dragon. It's really good. Have you ever thought of becoming an artist? I think you might have the talent for it. I couldn't forget that picture over the weekend. In fact, when I was looking at the fireworks on Saturday night, I saw some kind of strange fire-balloon, that looked just like your dragon. I don't know whether it really *was* like the dragon, or if I just saw it as a dragon, because I'd been looking at your picture. Your picture has got so much life in it, it made me see dragons all the way home!"

Peter looked at the picture. The dragon looked alive, and its eyes were glowing, but it looked small, and rather like a fish swimming in the water. It didn't look like the dragon he had ridden on Saturday night, full of power and fire.

"Can I paint another? A big one? A really big one?" he asked.

"Yes, if you like," said Mr. Brent. "I've got just the paper that might do for you."

He went to the cupboard, and took out a roll of dark blue paper. "How long do you want to make it?" he asked. "I can pin this all along the wall for you, if you like. It will give you a dark blue background, like the sky at night, and you can paint the dragon flying over the dark roof tops."

Mr. Brent rolled the paper along the pin board on the wall, and Peter stuck pins in to hold it in place. He was going to paint the dragon as big as he possibly could. He remembered every knob and bone along his back. If he shut his eyes, he could see the dragon again, sweeping along over the roof tops, his red eyes blazing, and waves of fire rolling out of his mouth.

Peter mixed up some paint, and began. He didn't even notice the others, as they settled down to their pictures. He knew he could do it. The dragon must be back in the mountains by this time, on the other side of the world. But he could paint a picture and then he would always have the dragon as he had seen it that night, flying over the city under the stars.

Peter filled his brush with ivory-coloured paint, and settled down happily to work.